Speedway Switch

BY JAKE MADDOX

illustrated by Sean Tiffany

text by Bob Temple

Librarian Reviewer
Chris Kreie
Media Specialist, Eden Prairie Schools, MN
MS in Information Media, St. Cloud State University, MN

Reading Consultant
Mary Evenson
Middle School Teacher, Edina Public Schools, MN
MA in Education, University of Minnesota

STONE ARCH BOOKS
Minneapolis   San Diego

Jake Maddox Books are published by Stone Arch Books,
A Capstone Imprint
151 Good Counsel Drive, P.O. Box 669,
Mankato, Minnesota 56002
www.capstonepub.com

Library of Congress Cataloging-in-Publication Data
Maddox, Jake.
    Speedway Switch / by Jake Maddox; illustrated by Sean Tiffany.
    p. cm. — (Impact Books. A Jake Maddox Sports Story)
    Summary: Quarter-midget car racer Michael Haynes and his twin
brother Mark, the team's mechanic, are used to winning their races, but
when a new, unscrupulous racer starts competing, even causing Michael
to be injured in a race, the twins are tempted to start using different
tactics themselves.
    ISBN-13: 978-1-59889-321-2 (library binding)
    ISBN-10: 1-59889-321-1 (library binding)
    ISBN-13: 978-1-59889-416-5 (paperback)
    ISBN-10: 1-59889-416-1 (paperback)
    1. Midget car racing—Fiction. 2. Automobile racing—Fiction.
3. Twins—Fiction. I. Tiffany, Sean, ill. II. Title.
PZ7.M25643Sp 2007
[Fic]—dc22   2006028023

Art Director: Heather Kindseth
Graphic Designer: Kay Fraser

Printed in the United States of America in Stevens Point, Wisconsin.
022011
006081R

Table of Contents

Michael Haynes squeezed the steering wheel as he roared around the bank. As the next straightaway turned into the other curve, his grip tightened.

The race was going fast. Only two laps were left. Michael couldn't see anyone in front of him. This was his chance to win.

Michael eased his quarter-midget car around the second turn and back toward the start line.

"Only two laps to go," he thought as his miniature race car crossed the line. "Just hold on. Don't blow it."

Michael had won races before. In fact, Michael had been one of the best racers at Mount Rose Speedway. He had zoomed through the beginner levels. He had graduated to junior-level racing last year.

When that season was over, Michael had won more races than any other driver. He was ready to move up to the senior level.

This season, however, had been different. A new racer, Buzz Shaw, had come to town for all of the big races in the season. Buzz's style of racing upset many of the boys on the senior level. He didn't seem to care if he banged up his car or got into an accident.

All he cared about was winning. He took big risks to get to the front of the pack. Sometimes those risks put other drivers in danger.

Some drivers, including Michael, thought that Buzz was causing other cars to run off the track on purpose. Michael thought Buzz was a dirty racer.

But Buzz's style, dirty or not, definitely helped him win.

Even when Buzz didn't cause an accident or take an unnecessary risk, his reputation made other racers fear him. Buzz used that to his advantage.

He had won every race he entered in the Mount Rose quarter-midget level.

Michael had come close to beating Buzz before, but he had never been able to.

Buzz had always done something on the last lap or two to make him win.

This time, Michael was in control. As he whipped a quick glance back, he didn't even see Buzz's car.

Another racer, Billy Watkins, was a few seconds behind. But Michael wasn't worried about him.

Finally, Michael was going to win a senior-level race. As he zoomed past the tower at the start line with only one lap to go, he felt the tension leave his body.

"I've got it," he thought. "This race is mine."

Michael shot a quick glance into the pits. He caught the eye of his identical twin, Mark, and flashed him a wink.

The look on Mark's face wasn't as confident. He was jumping up and down, pointing at something behind Michael.

As Michael headed into the second-to-last turn of the race, everything changed. That's when he felt it.

Thump.

(Chapter 2)

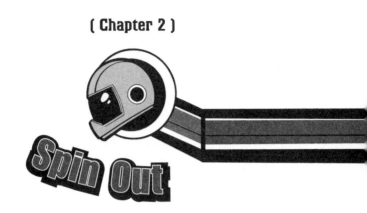

Spin Out

Michael felt the back end of his mini racer push out to the right. He knew right away he was in trouble. If he didn't control his car, he could spin out completely. Or worse, he could skid off the side of the track and hit the retaining wall.

Michael squeezed the steering wheel, as if he were strangling it. He jerked the wheel around to the right. He was trying to regain control of the car.

All he needed to do was get it headed straight down the track, and he'd be okay. He knew that Buzz was behind him, but there was only one turn left in the race. He could hold Buzz off and win.

But he only had a fraction of a second to keep the car headed down the track, and Michael overreacted. He turned the wheel too far back to the right. Instead of the right back end of the car spinning around, now the left side was moving forward.

In a flash, Michael was spinning. The car spun around twice before it stopped with two wheels lifted up in the air. For a split second, Michael thought the car might roll.

But the two wheels crashed back down on the ground with a loud smack!

Now Michael's car was facing the wrong way on the track. His engine had stopped. There was only one thing he could do. He had to sit and watch the other cars whiz past him, gunning for the finish line.

Michael looked across to the other side of the track, just in time to see Buzz Shaw cross the finish line first. Billy Watkins was second, and the other five racers zoomed in behind them.

Michael knew that when he walked over to the results board, he would see his own name in last place. Buzz had done it again.

Quick as lightning, Buzz pulled his car into the winner's circle. He unbuckled his shoulder harness and crawled out the side of the racer. He pried off his helmet and held it high above his head.

Michael couldn't get his car started again. When the car tipped sideways, the engine must have flooded, he thought. He was left sitting on the track.

Michael unbuckled his shoulder harness and crawled out. He'd have to get his brother to come help him push it out. Before he could do that, however, Michael had another problem.

Out of the corner of his eye, Michael saw Mark sprinting out of the pits. He was heading straight for the winner's circle. As Mark got close to Buzz and his crew, he started yelling.

"I saw that!" Mark was screaming. "I saw what you did! You rammed his bumper on purpose!"

Buzz didn't even raise an eyebrow.

"Get out of here, kid," he said. "You don't know what you're talking about."

But Mark didn't stop. "One of these times, you're going to really hurt someone," Mark continued. "You're going to get someone killed!"

Buzz let out a chuckle. "Just racin' to win, pal," he said. "Maybe your brother should come over to my place sometime. I could give him some lessons."

At that, Mark was ready for a fight. Michael ran over and arrived just in time to hold him back. "Mark!" Michael yelled. "Let it go. He's not worth it."

The brothers walked away, and the race judge handed the trophy to Buzz. Buzz held the trophy over his head, smirking as his family and crew cheered.

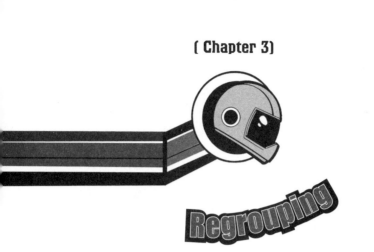

[Chapter 3]

Regrouping

Michael and Mark walked back toward the pits. Their father was there, waiting.

"Well, boys, that was a tough one," he said. "We'll get 'em next time."

"Tough one?" Mark muttered. "Buzz wrecked Michael on purpose!"

"You don't know that," Dad said. "Whatever happened, Michael will just have to do a faster time next time around, so Buzz can't catch up."

Michael frowned. "I don't know if he wrecked me on purpose, and I also don't know where he came from," he said. "I never even saw him coming."

Mark shook his head. "I saw the whole thing, Michael. He was about three cars back, and he just steamrolled people," Mark said. "He was cutting people off and running them toward the edges of the track, and all of a sudden, he was on your tail. Then he bumped you on purpose."

"All right, that's enough, boys," Dad said. "We've got to let this go and get back to the drawing board."

There was only one race left on the schedule for the summer season. It was the Mount Rose Grand Championship, the most important race of the year.

Buzz hadn't entered many races at Mount Rose during the season, because his family traveled around to many different tracks during the summer. But Buzz had won every race he'd entered, so he was in first place in the overall standings.

Michael knew he didn't have a chance to catch Buzz for the overall championship of the season. But he could still win the final race, and that would end the season on a good note.

To win, though, Michael knew he'd have to beat Buzz Shaw.

"How was the car?" Michael's dad asked. "Did it run okay?"

"Oh, yeah, the car was great," Michael said. "You guys did a great job."

Mark and Dad were Michael's pit crew. Dad kept an eye on everything, but Mark did most of the work on the car's engine and tires.

Mark had raced a little when he was younger, but he always liked the mechanical part more than the driving. Michael was exactly the opposite.

"Well," Dad said, "it looks like the car came out of the wreck okay. The engine was flooded a little, but it seems like it's okay now."

"I hope so," Michael said. "We've only got a week to get ready for the last race!"

Chapter 4

Michael and Mark spent the week getting ready for the final race of the summer. Michael took some practice runs on the track. Mark tuned up the engine with their father's help.

At night, when they lay in their beds at home, the boys talked strategy.

"There are forty laps in the race," Mark said. "Maybe you should hang back for a while. Then charge at him at the end."

Michael didn't like the sound of that. "Have you ever seen anyone catch Buzz from behind?" he asked. "No. If you try to pass him, he just blocks you off, even if it means running you off the track. I think the only way to beat him is to get a lead and never let up."

Both boys stared up at the ceiling of their room. They were thinking the same thing. No matter how they'd raced against Buzz in the past, nothing had ever worked. He had always found a way to cross the finish line first.

The night before the race, neither of them slept. They were both way too excited. It seemed like the morning would never come. As soon as their alarm went off, the boys ran in to wake their father.

At the racetrack, Mark and Dad made final tune-ups on the car. Michael did some stretching exercises, drank some water, and tried not to get too excited.

At noon, drivers started their qualifying runs. Each driver took six laps around the track, and their total time decided where they would start the race.

When it was Michael's turn, he pushed his car to its limits. He cut in close on the turns, and moved out wider on the straightaways. It was a great run.

Buzz's run was just as good. His car was always fast, and he seemed to have it in great control. All of his turns were clean.

By the time the qualifying runs were over, Buzz and Michael had the two best times of the day.

They would start the race at the front of the pack.

As race time neared, Michael's dad patted him on the back. Mark gave him a high five. Then Michael headed out to the track, where his car was waiting.

When he reached the car, Buzz was standing next to it. "Pretty nice car," Buzz said, pointing at Michael's blue and gold quarter-midget racer with the number 12 painted on the side. "Too bad it never gets a chance to finish first."

"This car's finished first plenty of times," Michael shot back.

"Not that I've ever seen," said Buzz with a smirk.

"Get ready," Michael said. "You might just see it today."

(Chapter 5)

Race to the Finish

Deep down, Michael wasn't nearly as confident as he was trying to sound. He just didn't want Buzz to think that he was scared. He wanted Buzz to know that he was serious about winning.

The race began with a pace car leading the racers on a couple of warm-up laps around the track. Then, as Buzz's and Michael's cars reached the starting line, the pace car pulled away.

The race began. Quickly, Buzz inched out in front.

Buzz had the lower track heading into the first turn. He took a sharp angle, holding the car close to the inside line.

That move forced Michael to take the longer, outside route. By the time the cars reached the first straightaway, Buzz's car was fully in front of Michael's.

Michael decided to make a quick move to get directly behind Buzz. His front bumper hugged the back of Buzz's car, just inches from touching it.

Michael wanted to try drafting, which he had seen professional drivers do. The driver would pull his car up close behind the car ahead, and let the front car fight the resistance of the wind.

It was a way to stay close without using as much energy as the front car did.

Mark saw Michael's move, and it surprised him. "We didn't talk about that!" Mark said to his father.

"Looks like a smart move to me," Dad said. "That's what the pros do."

For the first ten laps, Michael drafted off Buzz's car. Buzz didn't seem to mind. He liked being in front anyway.

The other racers were quickly falling behind. By the time Michael and Buzz reached the twentieth lap, they were almost a full lap ahead of the other cars.

Then Michael saw a chance. Buzz pulled up behind the slower cars on a straightaway. Then he tried to squeeze between two of them.

But the space wasn't big enough, and Buzz couldn't get through.

When Michael saw that, he moved out from behind Buzz. Instead, he went to the far outside position on the next turn.

It was a risky move. Going wide on a turn often caused drivers to fall back.

But Michael hit the gas hard and got around the turn ahead of one of the two cars that were pinching Buzz.

On the next straightaway, Michael pressed down hard on the gas pedal and cruised past two other slower cars.

And just like that, he was in front!

Buzz eventually forced his way between the two slower cars, but it was too late. Michael had the lead.

Michael knew that Buzz wouldn't stay behind him for long. He glanced back and could see that Buzz was closing up the space between them.

Buzz settled in close behind Michael. He had decided to do what Michael had done. Buzz was drafting.

Michael patiently held the lead. He wouldn't worry too much about Buzz until the final couple of laps. He knew that Buzz would wait until then to make his move.

A few minutes later, there were only two laps left in the race. It was time for Buzz to go for the lead.

Michael watched him carefully in the rearview mirror. He tried to figure out what Buzz's plan might be. How would Buzz try to take the lead?

Mark and his father were nervous. Mark was jumping up and down and yelling. He yelled so much that his voice was almost gone.

As the cars moved into turn two, Buzz went for it. At the turn, he eased back, creating a little room between him and Michael. Then, as Michael whizzed around the turn and into the straightaway, Buzz sped up. He moved close to Michael's car, trying to beat him to the next turn and force him away.

Michael wasn't letting up. He hit the gas hard and tried to force his way to the low spot at the next turn. But as the cars drew nearer to the turn, Buzz's car was next to Michael's. And he wasn't moving.

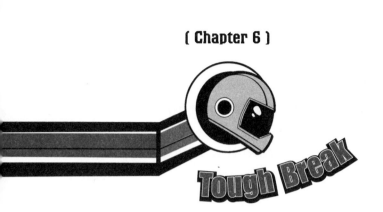

Buzz kept his car in the middle of the track instead of heading to the inside for the first turn on the final lap. That move kept Michael wide.

As they came out of turn one on the final lap, Buzz moved quickly toward the outside of the track.

Michael was stuck. He couldn't speed up fast enough to move ahead of Buzz.

If he slowed down, Buzz would surge past him and win the race. All Michael could do was try to hold his spot and hope Buzz didn't run him off the track.

It didn't work. Buzz kept pushing to the outside. Michael kept his foot pressed down hard on the gas pedal and tried to stay away from the wall.

But Michael's right front tire hit the wall. His car spun wildly away from the wall, smacking into Buzz's car and knocking it off the line.

Buzz lost control and was forced into the infield area. The bounce off Buzz's car caused Michael's racer to spin back into the main lane of traffic. Two other cars hit Michael's front end hard, and he felt a pain shoot up his right leg.

It was the worst pain he had ever felt.

From the seat of his car, Michael watched the rest of the race unfold. A little green car, Billy Watkins's car, made it through the tangle of wrecked cars and crossed the finish line first.

Buzz's car came to rest in the infield, and he never finished the race.

Michael unbuckled his shoulder harness, but he couldn't get out of the car. His leg hurt too badly.

He wasn't sure what had happened, and he couldn't bear to look down at his leg. It just didn't feel right, and Michael didn't know what he would see.

Mark and his father ran to the car. They were worried because Michael wasn't getting out.

Mark reached the car first. "What's wrong?" he asked. "What happened?"

"My leg," Michael said, reaching down.

Mark took a quick glance down at Michael's leg. His eyes grew wide and he stood up straight. "Dad!" he yelled. "Get the medic!"

Before Michael knew it, there was an ambulance on the track, and he was being helped onto a stretcher. They inflated an air cast around his leg and put him in the back of the ambulance.

Michael didn't know what to think. Everything was happening so fast. "Dad," Michael asked, "what's wrong with my leg?"

"It's broken," his dad said. "It's broken pretty badly, son."

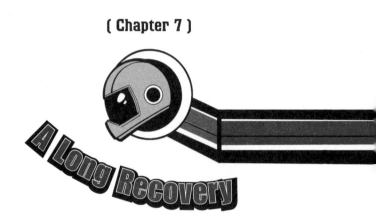

Chapter 7

A Long Recovery

At the hospital, the news wasn't any better. Michael's right leg was definitely broken, and he had torn some ligaments in his ankle, too.

The doctor broke the news to Michael, Mark, and their dad. Michael would have to have surgery on his ankle. Once the leg was healed, Michael would need a long period of physical therapy.

"I'm sorry, Michael," the doctor said.

"Injuries like this usually take a year or more to heal. You have to take it easy until it's ready."

Michael knew what that meant. He wouldn't be able to race in next summer's season.

Michael was heartbroken. "I can't believe I have to sit through another whole year of watching Buzz Shaw win all the races," he said.

His dad looked sad, and Mark reached out and gently patted Michael's arm. "At least you're okay," Mark said.

But Michael didn't see it that way. It didn't seem to him like he was okay at all. To Michael, it seemed like the end of the world.

After the surgery, Michael wore a cast that went all the way up to his knee.

Twelve weeks later, the cast was removed, and he was able to start his physical therapy exercises.

At first, Michael could barely put any weight on his leg. Over time, his strength grew. But he was still in a lot of pain, especially when he tried to test it by doing a little more than the doctors advised.

All Michael thought about that winter was racing.

He wanted so badly to heal fast enough that he could have even one race against Buzz. But every time he tried to suggest to his father that he be allowed to race, the answer was simple and direct.

"Not this year, Michael," his father would say.

Mark was just as unhappy.

No racing meant no working on the car's engine and tires. He and his dad repaired the damage from the accident. The number 12 car was looking brand new.

Once in a while, Michael would go out to the garage and get in the car. But that just made him feel worse.

One day, Michael's father came home from work and found Michael and Mark out by the car.

"Boys, I've been thinking," Dad said. "We've always been a team, right?"

"Right," the boys said.

"Well, Michael's hurt this year, but we can still be a team," Dad said.

The boys looked confused. "What do you mean?" Michael asked.

"Why don't you two just switch jobs?" Dad replied. "Mark, you can drive the car. And Michael, you can help me in the pits. We can still be Team Haynes!"

The boys looked at each other. They weren't sure what to say.

"But, Dad," Mark answered finally, "I'm not as good a driver as Michael is."

"And I'm not as good a mechanic as Mark is," Michael added.

"Look, boys," their dad said. "We can sit and watch Buzz win races all summer, or we can go out there and try to win some ourselves."

Smiles crossed the boys' faces. "Let's do it," Michael said.

"Yeah," Mark agreed. "Let's beat Buzz."

(Chapter 8)

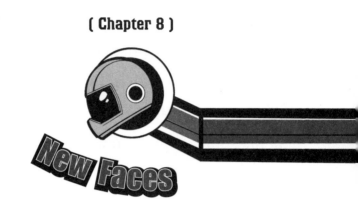

New Faces

As soon as summer came, Mark began practicing his driving skills at the track. Michael learned the mechanical side of things as quickly as he could.

They spent every weekend working on the car, but the new Team Haynes didn't start out very well.

Mark was never comfortable driving the car at its top speeds. Michael wasn't skilled at keeping the car running smoothly.

But by the time the first race of the season arrived, they were both more confident and were feeling better.

The first race was short, just twenty laps. Mark was very nervous before the race, and was quizzing Michael to make sure he had checked everything with the engine the way Mark would have done it.

Mark went through the qualifying runs and was set to run in the middle of the pack. That was better than he expected, but Michael wasn't happy.

"You've got to accelerate into the turns," Michael said. "Don't slow down. You'll never have a chance if you slow down going into the turns!"

Mark just smiled. "You need to relax," he said.

When the race started, Michael could barely stand still. The sound of the engines, the smell of the fumes, and the sight of Buzz leading the pack was too much. It was driving him crazy.

Mark got off to a good start. He passed a few cars in the first couple of laps. By the fifth lap, he was in third place.

But as the race moved on, Mark struggled to keep from getting passed. By the fifteenth lap, he was in last place.

Without Michael to challenge him, Buzz was pulling away for an easy victory.

On the final lap, he caught up to Mark. He pulled up alongside Mark, they made eye contact, and Buzz flashed a big grin.

Then Buzz passed Mark.

Michael felt his heart sink. It was almost more than he could take.

After the race, Team Haynes was a pretty unhappy crew.

"We'll use this as a learning experience," Dad said. "Don't worry, we'll get better as the year goes on."

He was right. Mark's performance improved in each race of the season, and Michael was doing a better job in the pits, too.

Still, Mark wasn't coming close to winning, and Buzz was winning whenever he raced.

During one race, Michael made a bad mistake on the engine that caused the car to fail in the middle of the race. It was a mistake Mark never would have made.

Buzz was on his way to another championship. After he won the second-to-last race of the year, Buzz had the championship pretty well wrapped up.

But the biggest race of the year still remained: the Mount Rose Grand Championship. It was the race that Michael had been injured in last year.

"If Buzz wins that race, too, it's going to be a long winter," Mark said one night. "But I don't think I can beat him."

Suddenly, Michael had an idea. "No, you probably can't beat him. But Mark Haynes can," Michael said, a grin coming across his face.

"What the heck are you talking about?" Mark said. "I am Mark Haynes."

"Are you?" Michael said. He smiled.

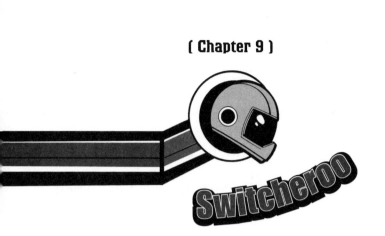

Chapter 9

Switcheroo

Mark stared at his brother. "I think that a year without racing has made you nuts, Michael! Are you losing your mind?" asked Mark.

"No, I'm not," said Michael. "Do you remember that April Fool's Day when we switched places in school?"

"Yeah," Mark said. "You went to my English class, and I went to your math class."

"Right," Michael said. "And no one noticed. Remember?"

"Yes," Mark said.

"So," said Michael, "let's do it again!"

A smile rolled across Mark's face. Then he frowned. "Wait a minute," he said. "If your leg feels good enough, why don't you just enter the race?"

"Dad would never let me," Michael said. "Trading places is the only way."

Mark agreed. "I'm in," he said.

* * *

Every day for the rest of the week, Mr. Haynes dropped off the boys and their car at the race track on his way to work. Michael and Mark didn't ever mention their plan.

At the track, Michael put on Mark's racing suit and ran his practice laps. He felt some pain in his leg, but the joy of being back on the track was more than enough to overcome it.

By the time the day of the championship came around, Michael was feeling comfortable in the driver's seat again. He barely even felt his leg. And Mark had made some changes to the engine, so the car was running better than ever.

On the morning of the race, Mr. Haynes checked the car over, and gave it a thumbs-up. The boys were dressed in their racing suits.

As they walked off toward the car, Michael yelled back to his dad.

"Hey, Dad," Michael said. "I'm going to watch this one from the stands, okay?"

"Sure," Mr. Haynes said.

Michael and Mark scurried off to the bathroom and changed racing suits. Most people, even those who knew them well, could only tell them apart by reading the names on their jumpsuits.

When they emerged from the bathroom, the first couple of people they ran into didn't notice they had switched. The plan was working!

The boys hurried to the car, and Michael jumped in. But as he was buckling himself in, he noticed a problem. Mr. Haynes was coming to the car!

(Chapter 10)

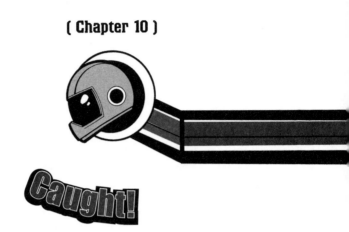

Caught!

Michael lowered the visor on his helmet. He hoped his dad wouldn't notice. Mark quickly started to walk away, hoping his dad wouldn't call to him. But it was too late.

"What's going on here?" Dad said as he approached the car.

"What do you mean?" Michael said from inside his helmet.

"Come on, boys," Dad said.

He laughed. "I'm not stupid. I can tell you apart from a mile away. I am your father, after all."

Michael and Mark were stunned. They couldn't believe they had been discovered. Now they were ready for a punishment, and they were both afraid it might mean neither of them would be allowed to race in the championship.

There was silence. All around them, racers were getting into their cars, buckling in, revving engines. But Team Haynes just stood in silence.

Finally, a grin came across Dad's face. "So, Michael," he said. "Your leg's feeling better?"

"Yes," Michael said. "It's not perfect, but it's good enough to race."

Mark opened his mouth, ready to beg. "Dad," he said, "please."

"Listen, boys," Mr. Haynes said. "Michael can race today. But if he's going to do it, we're going to do it right. Michael, get out of the car and go register for this race as yourself."

Michael didn't hesitate. In a flash, he was out of the car and running to the registration tent.

(Chapter 11)

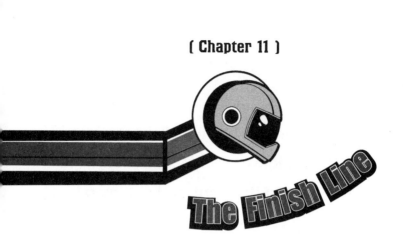

The Finish Line

Michael filled out the registration form, told the judge to scratch Mark Haynes from the race, and sprinted back to his car.

On the way, he passed Buzz Shaw.

"Ready to sniff my fumes again, Mark?" Buzz said.

"Actually, no," Michael said. "And I'm not Mark. It's me, Michael. I'm back."

Buzz's jaw dropped.

His face turned white. He struggled to get out another sharp comment, but Michael was already gone.

When the race began, Michael started from the middle of the pack. Rather than charge right to the front and challenge Buzz, Michael held back.

He passed a few cars and moved up to fourth place by the midway point of the race. Most importantly, his leg was feeling pretty good. Even if it did hurt, he was sure he wouldn't have noticed. He was racing, and that's all that mattered.

Mark cheered himself hoarse from the pits. Dad just stood there and beamed.

On the thirtieth lap, Michael made his charge. On a straightaway, he moved past two cars and into second place.

There, he hugged Buzz's back bumper and waited for his chance.

Everything inside him wanted to do exactly what Buzz had done to him. He wanted to get inside position and force Buzz off the track. But Michael knew he didn't want to win a race that way. He wanted to win fair and square.

The best way to do that, he decided, was to catch Buzz by surprise. So Michael decided not to wait for the last couple of laps to make a charge. With eight laps still to go, Michael made his move.

Coming around a curve, Michael did something odd. Instead of taking the shorter route and trying to cut inside Buzz on the straightaway, Michael headed for the outside.

Before Buzz realized what Michael was doing, they were running neck and neck. But Buzz still felt confident. He would do his usual trick and force Michael toward the wall.

Michael knew what was coming. He held his line and waited for Buzz to make his move. When he did, Michael hit the brakes for a split second. Buzz's car slipped to the outside lane as Michael dropped back. Then Michael hit the gas as hard as he could, driving toward the inside lane.

Confused, Buzz let off the gas for a second. By the time he hit it again, Michael was past him on the inside, heading for the lead.

Michael's move had worked. With six laps to go, he was in the lead! All he had to do now was hold Buzz off.

Michael made a fast decision. He was going to drive the car as hard as he could until the race was over. He was going to simply trust that all the work Mark had done on the car would make it hold up for six more laps.

Buzz tried several times to catch Michael, but he never could. Thanks to the great work of Team Haynes, Michael's car stayed true. And Michael's driving was flawless. As he rounded the final turn and headed for the finish line, Michael suddenly felt his leg throbbing.

But it didn't matter. Buzz was behind him, in second place, and Team Haynes had won the Grand Championship!

Michael took one extra spin around the track, pumping his fist in the air.

When he reached the winner's circle, his dad and Mark were already there. Michael jumped out of the car and walked confidently over to Mark. The twins gave each other a high five, and Mr. Haynes patted his boys on their backs.

When they turned to face the cheering crowd, they saw Buzz Shaw. He was walking out of the pits, shaking his head in disbelief.

About the Author

Bob Temple lives in Rosemount, Minnesota, with his wife and three children. He has written more than thirty books for children. Over the years, he has coached more than twenty kids' soccer, basketball, and baseball teams. He also loves visiting classrooms to talk about his writing.

About the Illustrator

When Sean Tiffany was growing up, he lived on a small island off the coast of Maine. Every day, from sixth grade until he graduated from high school, he had to take a boat to get to school. When Sean isn't working on his art, he works on a multimedia project called "OilCan Drive," which combines music and art. He has a pet cactus named Jim.

Glossary

harness (HAR-niss)—a series of straps that are designed to keep someone safe

overreact (oh-vur-ree-AKT)—to respond to something in an extreme way

plight (PLITE)—a situation in which there is great hardship

qualify (KWAHL-uh-fye)—to reach a level that allows you to do something

quarter midget (KWOR-tur MIJ-it)—a small race car, roughly one-fourth the size of a Midget racer, designed for children to use in racing

register (REJ-uh-stur)—to sign up for something

reputation (rep-yoo-TAY-shun)—your character, as viewed by other people

steamroll (STEEM-rohl)—to force your way over or past something or someone

straightaway (STRAYT-uh-way)—a stretch of a race track that is not curved

stretcher (STRECH-ur)—a flat bed used to carry an injured person

QUARTER-MIDGET RACING

Quarter-Midget racing is auto racing designed for kids. The small race cars are roughly one-quarter the size of a Midget racer, which is where the sport got its name.

There are Quarter-Midget racing associations all over the United States. Kids can start racing as young as age 5, and can race in Quarter Midgets until the age of 16. Many families work together as part of the racing "team," with parents working on the cars or timing races for their young racers.

Quarter-Midget cars can go 20-40 miles per hour, and they race on tracks that are usually 1/20th of a mile in length. The oval tracks can be made of dirt or pavement.

Young drivers usually start with training classes. Then they begin racing in Novice-level races. After moving up to Junior and Senior levels, many racers move up to the larger Midget cars.

Many of NASCAR's top drivers started out racing Quarter-Midget cars, including Jeff Gordon, Terry Labonte, Jimmy Vasser and Ryan Newman.

Discussion Questions

1. When Michael and his family realized that Buzz was racing dangerously, what could they have done to keep that from happening?

2. Why do you suppose Michael didn't protest Buzz's racing style to the racing judges?

3. Michael and Mark decided to switch places, trying to fool everyone, including their dad. What other things could they have tried to get Michael into the race?

4. Mr. Haynes let Mark do most of the work on the race car, and he just kept an eye on things. Why do you think he didn't fix the car himself?

Writing Prompts

1. Has there ever been a time in your life when you faced off against someone like Buzz? What happened? Write about it.

2. In this story, Michael tricked Buzz into trying to run him into the wall, then sneaked around the other side of Buzz to beat him. Can you write another ending for this story? How else could Michael have beaten Buzz?

3. Have you ever suffered an injury while participating in a sport? Write a story about it.

Internet Sites

Do you want to know more about subjects related to this book? Or are you interested in learning about other topics? Then check out FactHound, a fun, easy way to find Internet sites.

Our investigative staff has already sniffed out great sites for you!

Here's how to use FactHound:

1. Visit *www.facthound.com*

2. Select your grade level.

3. To learn more about subjects related to this book, type in the book's ISBN number: **1598893211**.

4. Click the **Fetch It** button.

FactHound will fetch the best Internet sites for you!